Karen's Movie

**Look for these
and other books about Karen
in the
Baby-sitters Little Sister series:**

Little Sister

Karen's Movie
Ann M. Martin

Illustrations by Susan Tang

A
LITTLE APPLE
PAPERBACK

SCHOLASTIC INC.
New York Toronto London Auckland Sydney

No part of this publication may be reproduced in whole or in part, or stored in a retrieval system, or transmitted in any form or by any means, electronic, mechanical, photocopying, recording, or otherwise, without written permission of the publisher. For information regarding permission, write to Scholastic Inc., 555 Broadway, New York, NY 10012.

ISBN 0-590-25996-2

12 11 10 9 8 7 6 5 4 3 2   5 6 7 8 9/9 0/0

Printed in the U.S.A.   40

First Scholastic printing, July 1995

*The author gratefully acknowledges
Stephanie Calmenson
for her help
with this book.*

A Perfect Summer Day

Gurgle. *Gurgle. Gurgle.* That was my tummy talking. I knew just what it was saying, too. It was saying, "Feed me! Feed me!"

I was lying in my bed looking out the window. It was a perfect summer morning. The sun was shining. The sky was blue. There was nothing I had to do except have fun. And feed my stomach. These were two good reasons to get up. So I did.

I am Karen Brewer. I am seven years old. I have blonde hair, blue eyes, and a bunch

1

of freckles. (In the summer I have a bunch and a half.) Oh, yes. I wear glasses. I have two pairs. I have a blue pair for reading. I have a pink pair for the rest of the time.

I also have a little brother. His name is Andrew. He is four going on five. He walked by my room on his way downstairs.

"Good morning, sleepyhead," said Andrew.

"Sleepyhead? Not me!" I said. I was dressed and downstairs in a flash.

Mommy had put out Krispy Krunchy cereal (my favorite), blueberries, milk, juice, and a basket of tiny rolls. My tummy was going to be gigundoly happy.

"These berries are delicious," said my stepfather, Seth. "They are as sweet as the berries on the farm."

Granny and Grandad, Seth's mother and father, live on a farm in Nebraska. I went there once to visit them all by myself.

"I have not talked to Granny and Grandad in a long time," I said. "I miss them."

2

"I am sure they miss you, too," said Seth. "We will call them later to say hello."

When we finished breakfast, Andrew and I went outside to play. One by one the other kids on our street came out to play, too.

"Hi, Karen. Hi, Andrew," called Nancy. Nancy Dawes lives next door to Mommy's house. She is one of my two best friends. My other best friend is Hannie Papadakis. She lives next door to Daddy's house. (Can you guess why I have two houses? I will tell you about that soon.)

Hannie, Nancy, and I call ourselves the Three Musketeers. That is because we like to do everything together. We are even in the same second-grade class at school.

Bobby and Alicia Gianelli came out next. Bobby is in our class at school, too. He used to be a bully. But he is not such a bully anymore. Alicia is Andrew's age. They are good friends.

Then Kathryn and Willie Barnes came

out. Kathryn is six and Willie is five.

There were eight of us all together. We always have a good time.

"Who wants to play Red Light, Green Light?" I asked.

Everyone wanted to play. Everyone wanted to be the traffic light, too. It is fun to be the traffic light. You get to call out "Red Light!" or "Green Light!" If you catch anyone moving when the light is red, you send them back to the starting line.

When we chose to see who would be the traffic light first, I was picked. Yes!

This was definitely turning out to be the perfect summer day.

Did You Guess?

If you guessed that I have two houses because my parents are divorced, you are right. Mommy and Daddy got divorced a long time ago.

When I was little we all lived together in one big house. It is here in Stoneybrook, Connecticut. Then Mommy and Daddy started feeling unhappy and fighting a lot. That made Andrew and me unhappy, too. Mommy and Daddy explained to Andrew and me that they loved us very much, but they did not love each other enough to stay married.

After the divorce, Mommy moved with Andrew and me to a little house not too far from the big house. Then she met Seth and they got married. That is how he became my stepfather.

Aside from the people at the little house, there are some pets. They are Midgie and Rocky, Seth's dog and cat; Emily Junior, my pet rat; and Bob, Andrew's hermit crab.

Daddy stayed at the big house after the divorce because it is the house he grew up in. He met someone new, too. Her name is Elizabeth. Daddy and Elizabeth got married and that is how Elizabeth became my stepmother. Elizabeth was married once before and has four kids. They are my step-sister and stepbrothers. They are Kristy, who is thirteen and the best stepsister in the world; David Michael, who is a little older than me; and Sam and Charlie, who are so old they are in high school.

I have one other sister named Emily Michelle. She is two and a half. Daddy and Elizabeth adopted her from a faraway country called Vietnam. I love Emily. That is why I named my rat after her.

Nannie lives at the big house, too. She is Elizabeth's mother. That makes her my stepgrandmother. Nannie is wonderful. She came to take care of Emily Michelle. But really she helps take care of everyone.

Here are the pets who live at the big house: Shannon, David Michael's Bernese mountain dog puppy; Boo-Boo, Daddy's cranky old tabby cat; Crystal Light the Second, my goldfish; and Goldfishie, Andrew's can-you-guess-what? (If you guessed a fish, you are right.) Emily Junior and Bob live at the big house whenever Andrew and I are there. We are there every other month.

Switching houses every month can be a problem if you are not organized. But we do not have too much trouble. I have a special name for Andrew and me. I call us Andrew Two-Two and Karen Two-Two. (I thought of that name after my teacher read a book to our class. It was called *Jacob Two-Two Meets the Hooded Fang*.) I call us that because we have two of so many things. We have two sets of clothes and toys and books, one set at each house. I have two bicycles and Andrew has two tricycles. I have two stuffed cats. Goosie lives at the little house. Moosie lives at the big house. And you already know about my two best friends, Nancy and Hannie. Plus, I have two mommies and two daddies, two cats and two dogs, two houses, and of course, two families.

Can you guess how I feel about being a two-two? Well, sometimes I am happy because it is fun to have two great families. But sometimes I feel a little sad because I miss one family when I am with the other. So if you guessed happy *and* sad, you are right.

You are very good at guessing.

8

Bad News

It was dinnertime on Tuesday. Seth had brought home watermelon for dessert. It was sweet and cold and very drippy. When I finished, I had pink juice on my white T-shirt, and a big pile of seeds on my plate. I moved them around until I had made a gigundoly wonderful picture. It was a watermelon seed dog with lots of spots.

"Taa-daa! This is my Dalmatian named Dotty," I said.

"She is terrific," said Mommy.

Ring, ring. Seth jumped up to answer the

phone. I hoped he would not talk for too long. We had tried to call Granny and Grandad the other day, but there was no answer. Seth promised we would try them again after dinner tonight.

I heard Seth say hello. He was quiet for a minute, then he said, "How is he? Is he going to be all right?"

Uh-oh. Something was wrong. Seth looked very worried. He was pacing back and forth. I started to worry, too. Who could he be talking about? Whom was he talking to?

Seth had turned the other way and was talking very softly, so I could not hear him anymore. When he hung up he came back to the table and sat down slowly.

"Everything is going to be all right," he said. "But I do have some bad news. That was Granny. She wanted us to know that Grandad is in the hospital."

"I am so sorry," said Mommy. "What happened?"

10

"Did he fall down and hurt himself?" asked Andrew.

"Did he break his wrist? I could tell him everything about broken wrists," I said.

I once broke my wrist roller skating. I had to go to the hospital. It was scary at first. But then it was not so bad.

"Grandad did not break his wrist," said Seth. "He had a heart attack. An ambulance came right away to help him and now he is out of danger. But it was a serious heart attack. He will be having bypass surgery on Friday."

An operation? This was very, very bad news. I love Grandad and I did not want him to be sick. I felt like crying.

"How is Granny doing?" asked Mommy.

"She is tired, but holding up okay. I told her I would come as soon as I can," said Seth. "I had better call the airline right away."

Seth picked up the phone again. He

made a reservation to fly to Nebraska on Thursday.

Then he called the hospital and asked to talk to the doctor who was taking care of Grandad.

After that he called Tia's family. Tia is the friend I made in Nebraska. She and her family are Granny's and Grandad's neighbors. Seth asked them please to look in on Granny until he arrived.

While Seth was on the phone, Mommy, Andrew, and I huddled together on the couch.

"I do not want Grandad to be in the hospital," said Andrew. "I am scared."

"The people in the hospital will take very good care of him," said Mommy.

I felt scared, too. I knew I would feel better if I did something helpful.

"We should make get well cards for Grandad," I said. "He can hang them in his hospital room."

"That is an excellent idea," said Mommy. "Why don't you bring your things in here?

I will clear the table. That way we can be together."

You know what? When Seth got off the phone we *all* made get well cards. We talked about Granny and Grandad and hospitals and operations and being sick.

By bedtime I was not so scared anymore. Everything was going to be all right. It just had to be.

Thoughtful Gifts

When I woke up on Wednesday, Seth was already on the phone.

"I am sure you are doing everything you can to make my father comfortable, Doctor Lerner. Please call me if there are any changes."

"How is Grandad?" I asked.

"The doctor says he is stable," Seth replied.

After breakfast we held a family meeting. Mommy and Seth decided that three weeks from Thursday Mommy would fly with Andrew and me to Nebraska. We would meet Seth there and visit with Granny and Grandad. The four of us would come back to Connecticut together on Sunday.

This was very exciting news. I hoped Grandad would be feeling much, much better by then.

"Will we see cows on the farm? And pigs and monkeys?" asked Andrew.

"Andrew. For heaven's sake. There are no monkeys on a farm," I replied. "Monkeys live in the jungle."

"I forgot. But will the other animals be there?" he asked.

Andrew was so excited. He had never been to visit Granny and Grandad in Nebraska. I told him about all the animals he would see.

"I will make some food to take along so Granny will not have to cook so much," said Mommy.

"I thought of a gift I would like to give my parents," said Seth. "I decided they might enjoy having a TV and VCR."

16

Oh, boy. I was not so sure. Grandad once told me they did not have a TV because they thought it was a waste of money. When I first arrived at the farm I was very unhappy without TV. Then I found other things to do. Fun things. I did not miss TV one bit.

"Do you really think they would like one? They never wanted one before," I said.

"I think that Grandad might be happy to have it while he is recovering from his surgery. He will not be able to get around and do the things he usually does," said Seth.

Then I remembered something important. Grandad told me they did not have cable on the farm. So he would not be able to see anything on TV even if he had one. I told Seth.

"You are right," Seth replied. "That is why I am getting the VCR. They can see movies on tape even if they do not have cable."

The next thing I knew, Seth was on the

phone again. "Hello, Howard. Can you deliver a TV and VCR to me today? I need them wrapped up and ready to ship to Nebraska tomorrow," said Seth.

Howard is Seth's good friend. He runs an appliance store. Whenever we need anything, we get it from Howard. Seth says Howard gives him a good discount.

Hmm. Seth's gift was very thoughtful. So was Mommy's. I wanted to take a thoughtful gift to Granny and Grandad, too. But what could it be? I thought and thought, but could not decide on anything.

Andrew and I went outside to play. When we came in for lunch, we were just in time to see the TV and VCR being delivered. Well, we saw the cartons anyway. Seth did not want to unpack them until he reached Nebraska.

All day I tried to think of a gift for Granny and Grandad. But I was stumped.

By bedtime, Seth was packed and ready to leave in the morning. I still had not thought of a gift. But I was not worried. I had three weeks to think about it.

I closed my eyes and thought hard about Granny and Grandad. Maybe if I thought hard enough, an idea would pop into my head while I was dreaming.

Eureka!

It was early Thursday morning. Mommy was getting ready to drive Seth to the airport. This was the day he was flying to Nebraska.

Ding-dong. I looked out the window. I saw Kristy on our front stoop. Yippee! Kristy was going to watch Andrew and me until Mommy returned from the airport. Kristy is an excellent baby-sitter. She is even president of a baby-sitting club she has with her friends.

"Hi, everybody," said Kristy.

20

I gave Kristy a big hug. Then it was time to say good-bye to Seth.

"See you in three weeks," said Seth. "Take care of each other while I am gone."

The first thing Kristy and Andrew and I did after Mommy and Seth left was make a big pitcher of lemonade. It always takes us a little while to get it just right. We squeezed lemons into a pitcher. We added water and sugar. Then we mixed it up and tasted it.

"Eww! Sour!" said Andrew, puckering his lips.

We added sugar, then tasted again.

"Pfooey. Sweet," I said.

Another lemon.

"Sour," said Kristy.

A pinch of sugar.

"Sweet," said Andrew.

A little water.

"Perfect!" we all said at once.

We cleaned up, then Andrew ran upstairs to play with his trucks. Kristy and I stayed in the kitchen and talked. I told Kristy all about my gift-for-Granny-and-Grandad problem.

"I want to take them something special. But I do not know what it should be," I said.

"How about something for their garden?" asked Kristy.

"They have so many things already. I do not know if they need anything else," I replied.

"What about a cookbook?" said Kristy.

"Granny and Grandad do not use cookbooks too much. They like to make up their own recipes."

"What are Seth and your mom giving them?" asked Kristy.

"They are giving them very thoughtful gifts. Mommy is making food so Granny will not have to cook. Seth is giving them a TV and VCR so they can watch movies while Grandad is recovering from his operation."

"Those really are thoughtful gifts," said Kristy.

Hmm. An idea was coming to me. If Seth was giving them a VCR to watch movies, they would need movies to watch.

"Eureka!" I cried.

"What? What did you think of?" asked Kristy.

"I thought of a perfect gift," I replied. "Daddy has a video camera. If he will let me borrow it, I can make a movie for Granny and Grandad to watch on their new VCR."

"That sounds great," said Kristy. "Sam could probably help you make the movie. He knows a little about filmmaking."

"I will be right back," I said. "I want to call Hannie and Nancy to tell them my idea. Maybe they will help me with the movie."

I called Nancy first.

"Guess what!" I said. "I am going to make a movie for my granny and grandad. Do you want to help?"

Nancy was excited. She said she would come over right away. I called Hannie next. She was excited, too. Her mom said she would drive her to my house.

I was gigundoly happy. I was about to begin my movie career.

Princess Gigglepuss

"What is the movie going to be about?" asked Hannie.

The Three Musketeers were in my room. We were holding our first movie meeting.

"I do not know yet," I replied. "But I think it should be funny. I saw a show on TV that said laughing is good for your health. That is just what Grandad needs."

"We could tell jokes," said Nancy.

"We could even act them out," said Hannie.

"Great idea!" I said.

I jumped up from the bed and started flapping my arms. I walked back and forth across my room like a chicken.

Hannie and Nancy were laughing.

"What are you doing?" asked Nancy.

"You mean you cannot tell? I am acting out a joke. Cluck, cluck, cluck!"

"I know, I know!" shouted Hannie. "Why did the chicken cross the road?"

"To get to the other side!" replied Nancy.

"Right," I said.

We took turns acting out jokes. But we decided that a good movie needs more than jokes. It needs a story.

"Let's put a princess in our story," said Nancy.

"She could be a funny princess who tells jokes," I said.

"We could have three funny princesses," said Hannie. "The funniest one gets to marry the prince."

I ran to my desk to get paper and a pencil.

"It is time to write our script," I said. "Hey! I just thought of a title."

I wrote it in big letters for Hannie and Nancy to see.

PRINCESS GIGGLEPUSS

"I love it!" said Hannie.

"Me, too," said Nancy. "Let's start writing."

Here is what we wrote.

PRINCE: Mother and Father, I am looking for a princess to be my bride. I want a bride who can make me laugh.

KING: Do not worry, my son. We will put a notice in the royal paper. We will find you a princess right away.

NARRATOR: One week later, a girl knocked at the palace door. The prince asked the girl to make him laugh.

GIRL NUMBER ONE: Why did the firefighter wear red suspenders?

PRINCE: To keep his pants up. Ho-hum.

NARRATOR: The girl was sent away. Later that day, a second girl knocked at the palace door. The prince asked her to make him laugh.

GIRL NUMBER TWO: Knock-knock.

PRINCE: Who is there?

GIRL NUMBER TWO: Little old lady.

PRINCE: Little old lady who?

GIRL NUMBER TWO: I did not know you could yodel!

PRINCE: Ho-hum. I have heard that before.

NARRATOR: The second girl was sent away. Early that evening . . .

Suddenly I heard Mommy's voice. She was back from the airport.

The Three Musketeers ran downstairs to meet her. I told Mommy about the movie for Granny and Granddad.

"I am sure they will love it," she said. "Did Daddy say you could borrow his camera?"

Uh-oh. I had not asked him yet. What if

he said no? "I will call him right now," I said.

I told Daddy about Grandad and the VCR and my movie. Then I asked if I could borrow his camera. Guess what. He said, "No problem." He even put Sam on the phone. Sam promised to help us with the movie.

"Come on," I said to Hannie and Nancy. "We have a movie to write."

Casting Call

I woke up on Friday morning feeling very happy.

"I am making a movie. My very own movie," I told Goosie.

I thought Goosie gave me a funny look when I told him it was my very own movie. I guess that is because he saw Hannie and Nancy helping me write it the day before.

"Yes, I know Hannie and Nancy helped me. But they had to go home before the story was finished. So I wrote the ending all by myself. Besides, the movie was *my* idea and it is for *my* grandad," I said.

I did not have time to sit around explaining things to Goosie. I had told the kids in my little-house neighborhood to be in my backyard at ten o'clock sharp if they wanted to be in the movie. (Hannie was coming, too, even though she lives near the big house. Her mommy was going to drop her off.)

At five minutes to ten, Andrew and I went out to the backyard. Nancy, Kathryn, and Willie were there. Bobby and Alicia were hurrying down the street. And Hannie's mommy was pulling into the driveway.

As soon as we were all together, I said, "Welcome to the casting call for *Princess Gigglepuss.*"

I read the script out loud from beginning to end. I used a different voice for each character. I thought I did a very good job. At the end, everyone clapped.

"Thank you," I said. "I will now assign parts."

"Wait a minute," said Bobby. "Who made you boss?"

"Um, well, the movie is for my grandad. So I have to make sure everything comes out okay. That is why I am going to be the director," I said.

"What part do I have?" asked Bobby.

"You are the cameraman. You get to film the movie. My brother, Sam, will help you."

"Cool!" said Bobby.

I could see Bobby did not mind my being boss anymore.

"Hannie, you will be girl number one. Nancy, you will be girl number two. Alicia will be girl number three," I said.

"What about me?" asked Andrew.

"You will be the prince. That is a big part. But I will help you practice."

That left Kathryn and Willie.

"Kathryn, you will be the narrator. The narrator tells what is happening whenever the actors are not talking," I said. "And Willie, you will be the king."

That was it. Everyone had a part.

Woof! Woof! Midgie was running in circles, wagging her tail. I guess she wanted to be in my movie, too.

"Okay, Midgie. You can be the royal watchdog," I said. "Does anyone have any questions? No? Good."

I did not give anyone a chance to ask anything. That is because I wanted to run through the movie. I wanted to see everyone in action so I could think about their costumes.

"I only have one copy of the script now. I will hold it up when it is your turn to read. If you do not know how to read yet, I will help you say your part."

"Where is my camera?" asked Bobby.

"I do not have it yet. You can make believe you are filming. It will be very good practice," I said. "Okay, everyone. *Princess Gigglepuss.* Take one."

The Phone Call

It was late Friday afternoon. I was helping Mommy fix dinner. (I was washing lettuce for our salad.)

Ring, ring.

"That might be Seth," said Mommy. "He promised to call us from the hospital after Grandad's surgery."

It was Seth. Mommy talked to him for awhile. Then she passed the phone to me.

"Hi, Seth. How is Grandad feeling?" I asked.

Seth told me that the surgery went as

well as could be expected. Grandad was going to get better. But the doctors did not know how long it would take.

"And he may never feel as good as he did before the heart attack," said Seth.

"I am working on a surprise gift for him," I said. "I think it will help him get better fast."

When I finished talking to Seth, Granny got on the phone.

"What is this about a surprise for Grandad?" she asked.

"I cannot tell you what it is because it would not be a surprise anymore. And it is for both of you," I added.

I talked to Granny a little more. Then it was Andrew's turn. When he finished, I talked to Seth again.

"I forgot to tell you that Midgie is going to be part of the surprise," I said.

Seth thought that was very mysterious. I wanted to tell him more, but someone at the hospital was waiting to use the phone. So we had to say good-bye.

After the phone call, Andrew and I decided to write to Grandad. When you are in the hospital you need all the cheering up you can get.

I found my artist's supplies. I have all kinds of paper, colored markers, glitter, and glue.

Andrew found some old magazines. He cut out pictures of things Grandad likes and pasted them on paper to make a get well card.

I was going to write Grandad a letter. First I made a beautiful glitter border. At each corner I drew a heart. That left plenty of room in the middle to write.

DEAR GRANDAD,
    HOW ARE YOU? ARE THEY BEING
NICE TO YOU AT THE HOSPITAL?
    I AM GLAD YOUR SIRGERY IS OVER.
I AM WORKING ON A SPECIAL GIFT
FOR YOU. IT IS A CHEERING-UP GIFT.
ANDREW AND ALL MY FRIENDS ARE

HELPING. EVEN MIDGIE IS HELPING. I
WILL SEE YOU IN LESS THAN THREE
WEEKS. I CAN HARDLY WAIT. I MISS
YOU!
GET WELL SOON!!!

LOVE, KAREN

Dress Rehearsal
Number One

I held a movie meeting at the little house on Monday morning.

"First of all, I have scripts for everyone. Please take them home and learn your lines," I said. (Mommy had made copies for me at the post office.)

"Second of all, it is time to make our costumes. I worked very hard over the weekend and made pictures of the costumes everyone will wear."

I passed out the pictures I had drawn.

The costumes were very fancy with ruffles and sequins and feathers.

"I wish you had told me you were working on costumes," said Nancy. "I would have helped you."

"Me, too," said Hannie.

They both sounded a little grumpy. I did not understand why. Their costumes were going to be very beautiful.

I spread out everything we needed on the kitchen table. There was cardboard for crowns and crepe paper for ruffles. There were brown paper bags and old pillowcases. (All we had to do was cut holes for heads and arms.) And there was a big box of dress-up clothes with hats, jewelry, scarves, and a feather boa that Mommy once gave me.

"Let's get busy!" I called. "If anyone needs help, just let me know."

I went to work on my costume. Then I noticed that no one was asking for help. I walked around the room and looked over everyone's shoulder the way my teacher does at school sometimes.

"Very nice, Willie," I said. "Alicia, a little less glue on your crown. Kathryn, more ruffles please."

We worked on our costumes Monday and again on Tuesday. By Wednesday we were ready for a dress rehearsal. I was gigundoly excited.

"Places, everyone!" I said. Then I realized I had not told them where their places were yet. That was an important job for the director.

"Kathryn, you stand here," I said. "Andrew, over here. Hannie and Nancy, you have to wait off to the side until I tell you to come in."

"We know that, Karen," said Hannie. "You do not have to tell us."

"A director's job is to give direction," I said.

"If we want directions, we will look at a map," said Bobby. (He thought that was very funny.)

"All right, everyone. Quiet on the set. This is dress rehearsal number one for *Princess Gigglepuss* by Karen Brewer," I said.

"Ahem!" said Hannie.

"Double ahem," said Nancy. "You forgot about us."

"I did not think you would mind," I said. I started over. "This is dress rehearsal number one for *Princess Gigglepuss* by Karen Brewer with a little help from her friends, Hannie and Nancy. Andrew, please begin."

"Do I have to go first?" asked Andrew.

"Yes, you have to go first. You are the prince," I replied.

"Okay," said Andrew. " 'Mommy and Daddy, I am looking for . . .' "

"Cut!" I yelled. "You are not supposed to say 'Mommy and Daddy.' You are supposed to say 'Mother and Father.' Please begin again."

" 'Mother and Father, I . . . I am . . .' I am all mixed up now," said Andrew.

"Andrew, you were supposed to practice

your lines," I said. I stamped my foot. (I once saw a director do that.)

"You should not be mad at Andrew. He is only little," said Nancy.

Oh, boy. Dress rehearsal number one was not going the way I wanted it to. This might be a long day.

Lights! Camera! Action!

We rehearsed for two more days. On Thursday morning, Sam came to the little house and gave Bobby important tips about using the camera. By Thursday afternoon, we were ready to film.

"Places, everyone!" I called.

I decided to make a few small changes before we began.

"Andrew, please move to the right. Willie, that means you have to move back. You, too, Alicia," I said.

"I like where I was before," said Andrew.

"It is better this way. Quiet on the set,"
I said. "Lights! Camera! Action!"

Bobby turned on the camera and started filming. I announced the title, then Andrew began.

" 'Mother and Father, I am looking for a princess to be my bride,' " said Andrew. " 'I want a bride who can make me laugh.' "

"Cut!" I yelled.

"Andrew, please look at Willie," I said.

"But I want to look at the camera," said Andrew.

"I am the director and I say you have to look at Willie," I replied.

Andrew stuck his tongue out at me. But he looked at Willie. Then it was Willie's turn.

"I do not want to wear ruffles anymore," said Willie. "They are itchy. And girls wear ruffles."

"Kings wear ruffles, too," I said.

"They do not," said Willy.

"They do, too. If you do not wear ruffles,

then you cannot be in my movie."

Willy left his ruffles on.

Kathryn's line came next. Then came Hannie's.

" 'Why did the firefighter wear purple suspenders?' " said Hannie.

"Cut!" I yelled. I noticed that the camera was still running. I could not understand why. I looked at Bobby and he turned it off.

"The script says red suspenders, not purple," I told Hannie.

"Purple is funny," said Hannie. "And you are being too bossy."

"Directors are bossy. The suspenders are red," I said.

Nancy's line came next. Right in the middle of her knock-knock joke, she started to laugh.

"Cut!" I called again. "You are not supposed to laugh. You did not laugh yesterday."

"I am laughing because I am nervous," said Nancy.

"Well, there is no laughing allowed," I said.

We had to film Nancy's part three times to get it right. Then Kathryn read her line.

" 'Early that evening, there was another knock at the palace door,' " she said.

Midgie was supposed to bark then. But she was watching a squirrel in a tree. Oh, well. The show must go on. It was time for Alicia's line.

" 'I am here to make you laugh,' " she said.

" 'Are you going to tell a funny joke?' " asked Andrew.

" 'No,' " Alicia replied.

" 'Are you going to sing a funny song?' "

" 'No.' "

" 'How will you make me laugh?' "

" 'Like this!' " Alicia tickled Andrew with a feather boa.

" 'Ha! Ha! Ha! I want you for my bride,' " said Andrew.

" 'And so they were married and lived

happily ever after,' " said Kathryn. " 'The end.' "

"Cut!" I called.

"Yippee!" said Willie.

"Hooray!" said Kathryn. "Who wants to play tag?"

My cast and crew waved good-bye. In a flash, they were gone.

We Quit!

Later, while Andrew was playing in his room and Mommy was cooking dinner, I decided to look at some of my movie. I popped Bobby's videotape into the VCR, rewound the tape, and sat back to watch it. (All I needed was popcorn.)

I was very excited when I saw myself on TV.

" 'Princess Gigglepuss by Karen Brewer with a little help from her friends, Hannie and Nancy.' "

Wow, I thought. I did that really well.

" 'Mother and Father, I am looking for a princess to be my bride. I want a bride who can make me laugh.' "

Hmm. Andrew sounded pretty good. But Bobby had shot only half of Willie. Half a person looks silly on the screen. We would have to shoot that scene again.

I watched a little more. Suddenly I heard something strange. I rewound the tape. I heard it again. It sounded like someone sneezing, someone who was not in front of the camera. I had not noticed that before. I must have been too busy directing. We would have to reshoot that scene, too.

When I reached Hannie's part, I was not too happy. I did not like the way she said "red suspenders." I think she was mad at me for not letting her say purple. That is one more scene to reshoot, I thought. A director's work is never done.

The next day when everyone was outside, I made an announcement.

"Hey, everyone, listen up. I watched a little of the movie last night. We need to shoot a few scenes over again," I said.

"Oh, no!" said Kathryn.

"I do not want to," said Andrew. "I want to play."

"Come on, everyone," I said. "We want to make a great movie, right?"

"Oh, all right," said Bobby. "But only if it does not take a long time."

We went back to the little house and put on our costumes. Bobby got the camera and we went outside to reshoot three scenes.

"Problem number one," I said. "Bobby, you cut Willie in half. Half a person on the screen looks very silly."

"Sorry, Ms. Director," said Bobby.

We reshot the scene. I stood Andrew, Willie, and Alicia where they had been standing during the dress rehearsal. I guess I had moved them too far apart when Bobby was filming them the day before. But I did not tell anyone that.

"Problem number two," I said. "Somebody sneezed. No one is allowed to sneeze or cough or make any noise."

"Achoo!" said Nancy.

"Very funny," I said.

We reshot the second scene. I listened carefully to make sure no one made noise.

"Problem number three," I said. "Hannie, you sound grumpy when you say 'red suspenders.' Please try to be more cheerful."

"That does it!" said Hannie. "I cannot sound cheerful because I do not feel cheerful. All you are doing is bossing everyone around and complaining. I quit!"

"Making this movie was supposed to be fun. But thanks to you it is not," said Nancy. "I quit, too."

"Me, too," said Alicia.

"We all quit!" said Bobby.

Everyone threw down their costumes and stomped off.

Oh, well. I had enough film to make my movie for Grandad. That was what mattered most.

Bossy

On Saturday, Mommy drove me to the big house. Sam was going to help me edit my movie. I raced inside.

"Hi, everybody!" I said.

"Hi, honey. How is your movie coming along?" asked Daddy.

"I think it is going to be very good. Are there Academy Awards for homemade movies?"

"Come on," said Sam. "I want to see this award-winning show."

Sam and I went into the TV room to

watch *Princess Gigglepuss*. I had watched only a little of it the day before. This was the first time I was going to see the whole thing.

"Hey, you look cool on TV," said Sam when he saw me.

"Thank you!" I replied.

I thought the movie looked pretty good up to the part in which Hannie asks the firefighter riddle. Then I got a surprise.

I saw myself yelling, *"Cut!"* I was looking straight into the camera at Bobby, and he was filming me.

A minute later I saw myself yelling, *"Cut!"* again. Then I saw myself telling Nancy she was not supposed to laugh.

"You are a pretty tough director," said Sam.

Hmm. I guess I did act kind of bossy. But I had to. A director must take charge. Hannie was supposed to say "red," not "purple." Nancy was not supposed to laugh when she said her lines. Someone had to tell them these things. And I was the director, so that someone had to be me.

We watched the first day's filming and then we saw the parts that we had reshot.

"The scenes you reshot are a big improvement," said Sam. "I kind of miss the sneezing in the background, though."

I giggled.

We watched the tape again from the beginning. This time I told Sam exactly which parts of the tape I wanted for the movie and the order they needed to be in.

"No problem," said Sam. "Um, did you want me to leave in the parts where you are yelling at everyone? Or should I take them out?"

"You are very funny," I said. "Please take them out."

"I will have to work on this at the high school," said Sam. "There is plenty of editing equipment there. But they are running a summer workshop, so I will have to wait my turn."

58

"Will it be ready by the time I go to Nebraska? I am leaving a week from Thursday," I said.

"I promise to have the tape for you before you leave," said Sam. "And I will make a copy of it for you to keep here."

Daddy poked his head into the room then.

"Are you ready to join us for some lunch?" he asked.

My work as a movie director was done. The videotape would be ready for my trip to Nebraska. Lunch sounded like a very good idea.

"We are on our way," I replied.

Nebraska, Here I Come!

"Hi, Granny," I said. "I wish we were in Nebraska already. I can hardly wait to see you."

It was Wednesday, the day before our trip. Mommy, Andrew, and I were taking turns talking on the phone with Seth and Granny. Grandad was getting better. But he was still in the hospital.

I talked to Granny awhile longer. Then I passed the phone to Andrew and went upstairs to pack. The first time I went to Nebraska, I packed dress-up clothes. This time

I knew better. I put in some pants, shirts, and sneakers. Then I found the overalls and straw hat that my friend Tia had helped me pick out. I would probably end up wearing them most of the time I was there.

I put the straw hat on my head and looked in the mirror.

"Nebraska, here I come!" I said.

"Karen, what is there to do in Nebraska?" asked Andrew. He was standing at my door.

"There are lots of things to do," I replied. "We will feed the chickens, and pick vegetables from the garden. We can read and play in the hayloft. And we will go to visit Tia on her farm. Then we will get to see my chick. Remember I told you I watched chicks hatch from their eggs? Oh, yes. We will see Pearl the cat, and Sheppy the dog. We are going to have so much fun!"

"Will the plane ride be fun?" asked Andrew.

"Oh, definitely. Mommy said she will

61

make each of us a Fun Bag. Seth made one for me when I flew to Nebraska by myself. He put crayons, a coloring book, pencils, paper, and books to read in it. But we will probably sit next to very nice people and they will talk to us the whole time," I said.

Mommy joined us upstairs.

"How are you two doing with your packing?" she asked.

"I am doing fine," I replied. "I am almost finished."

"I have not started yet," said Andrew.

"Come, I will help you," said Mommy.

When Mommy and Andrew left, I did some more packing. Glasses. Toothbrush. Hairbrush. Books. Videotape. (Sam had dropped off the videotape the day before. It was gigundoly great!)

I was tired of packing. I wanted to call Hannie and Nancy and tell them about my trip. But ever since we finished the movie, they had been acting very busy. I think they did not want to talk to me. Come to think of it, I had also not seen Bobby, Alicia, Kathryn, or Willie much since we finished the movie.

"Hey, Goosie. You are not mad at me, are you? No? Good," I said.

I took off my hat and rested it on Goosie's head. Goosie had traveled with me the first time I visited Nebraska. He liked it so much I promised he could go again.

We Made It!

"Rise and shine!" I said. "We are going to Nebraska!"

I was the first one up on Thursday morning. I woke Mommy and Andrew. Then I got dressed.

The last time I was on a plane, the flight attendants were all wearing navy blue. So I put on my blue leggings and T-shirt. I found my pin shaped like flying wings and pinned it to my shirt. (A very nice pilot gave it to me.)

Mommy, Andrew, and I ate breakfast. Then we loaded the car and headed for the airport.

Andrew and I sang "Old Macdonald Had a Farm." Only we changed the words to "Granny and Grandad had a farm."

Next we counted all the license plates with the letter A. Whoever reached ten first won. I won the first game. Andrew won for the letter B. We were up to the letter G when we started seeing planes flying overhead.

"I see the airport, Mommy!" Andrew cried. "Hurry!"

"We have plenty of time," Mommy replied.

We did not have so much time after all. The line at the check-in counter was very long and slow. Someone was having a problem with a ticket. While we waited, Andrew and I watched planes taking off and landing. Mommy tapped her foot and looked at her watch a lot.

Finally it was our turn. It was a good thing, too, because our flight was being announced.

"Flight number one-oh-eight to Omaha now boarding at gate six."

"Hold hands now," said Mommy.

We raced through the airport to our gate. People jumped out of our way as we passed. It was exciting.

By the time we found our seats we were huffing and puffing. I got to sit near the window. Andrew was in the middle. Mommy sat on the aisle. I decided it was my job to help Andrew since I am an airplane expert.

"It is very important to buckle up," I said to him. "Just like in a car."

Then I reminded him what all the little buttons over our seats were for.

"This button is for the light. This one makes air blow on you. And if you press this button, a very nice person will come and help you," I said.

A flight attendant made a little speech

about safety as the plane started to roll down the runway. I thought Andrew might be nervous so I held his hand. The plane started moving faster and faster. Then it started to rise.

"Cool!" said Andrew. He let go of my hand and leaned over to look out the window. There were big puffy marshmallow clouds in the sky.

The ride sped by. Andrew and I played with puzzles from our Fun Bags. Then the flight attendants brought around lunch. The food was not too tasty. But I liked opening all the little packages.

After lunch I felt sleepy. The next thing I knew, the airplane was bumping along the ground. We had arrived in Nebraska.

"Hi, Seth! We made it!" I called.

Seth was at the gate waiting for us. He gave us each a big hug.

"I am so happy to see you. Granny and Grandad are looking forward to seeing you, too," said Seth.

We drove to the farm in Granny's and Grandad's rusty green and white pickup truck. When we pulled up to the house, Sheppy came running to greet us, his tail wagging.

"Hi, Sheppy. This is my brother, Andrew. He came all the way from Stoneybrook to see you," I said.

Pearl the cat was peeking out at us from the barn.

"I see cows and pigs, too!" said Andrew.

"The chickens are over there. We will have to feed them in the morning. And we will pick vegetables from the garden for dinner every night," I said.

There was so much to do. I only wished our vacation could last longer. But I did not want to waste time wishing. It was time to start having fun!

The Farm

I raced into the farmhouse.

"Hi, Granny! We are here!" I called.

"Granny is not home," said Seth. "She is at the hospital with Grandad. In fact, I will be leaving in a few minutes to join them."

"Can we go with you to see Grandad?" I asked.

"I am sorry but you cannot. He would love to see you both. But children under twelve are not allowed to visit at the hospital," replied Seth.

I knew all about that rule. The hospital in Stoneybrook had the same one. I was not allowed to visit Nancy when she went to the hospital to have her appendix taken out.

"Why don't you show Andrew around the farm?" said Seth. "Granny and I will be back before you know it."

"I have to stay inside to be near the phone," said Mommy. "Please be sure you do not bother the animals. And do not go near any machinery."

Well, boo and bullfrogs. It sounded like we could not do much at all. Too bad for Andrew. When I was on the farm with Granny and Grandad I got to do lots of things.

"I want to find Sheppy," said Andrew.

Andrew did not seem to mind that we could not do much. He was just happy to be on the farm.

We found Sheppy by the cow pasture. Andrew ran to him and leaned against the fence.

"Do not get too close to the cow," I said.

When Granny and Grandad were here, I could pet the cow. But I did not think Mommy would want us to do that.

Moo-oo!

"I think the cow is happy to see me," said Andrew.

We watched the cow for a few minutes. She mooed. She chewed on grass. She swished her tail to swat the flies off her back. I did not think this was very exciting.

We looked at the pigs next.

"They do not look like the Three Little Pigs in my storybook," said Andrew. "Those pigs are pink."

"No. These are different colors. And they are hairy, too," I said. "Come on. I will show you the brooder house. When Granny and Grandad need more chickens, they put eggs in here. It is warm so the eggs can hatch."

We went into the brooder house. There were some eggs inside. But nothing was happening. Waiting for eggs to hatch is boring. It is only fun when the chicks start poking through their shells. The last time I was here, I got to see my very own chick, Tia, hatching. (I named her after my friend Tia.)

Crash! The noise came from the barn. Goody. Finally something exciting was happening.

"Let's go!" I said.

But by the time we reached the barn, it was quiet. Pearl was sitting up on a shelf looking down at us. There was a pile of cans on the ground below her.

"She must have knocked them down when she jumped up there," I said.

"Wow! Look at that tractor," said Andrew.

The tractor was parked at the side of the barn. I did not know why Andrew was so excited. He could only look at the tractor. When Grandad was here, I got to ride it. I even got to steer by myself. I guess Andrew was having fun because everything was new to him.

I had seen it all before. I wondered how much longer it would be before Seth and Granny came home.

"Karen! Andrew! Grandad is on the phone," called Mommy.

We raced inside the house to talk to Grandad.

"How are you feeling?" I asked.

Grandad said he was feeling a whole lot better.

"I have some good news," he said. "I will be coming home on Saturday."

Saturday? That was the day after tomorrow. Yippee!

Visiting Tia

I was up in the hayloft with Andrew. We had just finished dinner. Seth and Granny had come home to eat with us. Then Mommy went back to the hospital with Seth. It was always two grown-ups with Grandad and one grown-up with us. I wanted us all to be together.

I closed my eyes and crossed my fingers.

"What are you doing?" asked Andrew.

"I am wishing for Saturday to come really fast," I replied. "Then Grandad will be home."

My wish did not come true right away. The night went by as slow as molasses. The morning was even worse. We had fun feeding the chickens. But the rest of the time we just walked around looking for something to do.

Finally in the afternoon, Granny came to our rescue.

"I guess I can leave the phone long enough to drive you to Tia's house," said Granny. "How does that sound?"

It sounded gigundoly great!

When we arrived at Tia's farm Granny beeped the horn on the pickup. Tia came running out to see who was honking. She looked just the same. Her hair was cut very short. She was wearing overalls and a blue shirt. I used to think she looked like a boy. Now I thought she looked like Tia.

We were very excited to see each other again. We kept jumping up and down and shouting.

"I will pick you up a little later," called

Granny over the noise. "Have fun."

I stopped jumping and shouting long enough to introduce Tia to Andrew.

Then I asked about my chick. I had given the chick to Tia to take care of. I thought my chick would be much happier living on a farm than in a house in Stoneybrook, Connecticut.

"Come, I will show her to you," said Tia. "Only she is not a little chick anymore."

"What is she now?" asked Andrew. "An elephant?"

I could tell this afternoon was going to be fun.

The three of us walked to the chicken coop.

"There she is," she said.

I could hardly believe my eyes. Tia was pointing to a beautiful full-grown hen.

"Thank you for taking such good care of her," I said.

Tia gave Andrew a tour of her farm. But on this tour we could do things. Tia's dad gave us each a ride on the tractor. We patted the cows. Then while Andrew played fetch with Tia's dog, Hank, Tia and I sat in the hayloft and talked about all the things that had happened since we last saw each other.

Before we knew it, Granny was beeping the horn on the pickup truck again. Boo and bullfrogs. The afternoon had gone too fast.

Welcome Home, Grandad!

The next morning whizzed by, too. That is because we were busy getting ready for Grandad to come home.

"Pass the scissors, please," I said to Andrew.

We had written the words *WELCOME HOME* in great big letters and colored them in. We were cutting out each letter for Mommy to string up across the front yard fence. This would be a very good sign for Grandad to come home to.

Seth said that Grandad would not be able

to climb stairs yet. So we made the downstairs den into a cozy room for him. Mommy opened the couch and put pretty sheets on the mattress. Andrew drew pictures of the farm animals for Grandad to look at in case he could not go outside to visit them. Seth set up the TV and VCR so Grandad could watch it from his bed. And I put a beautiful bouquet of flowers in a vase because Grandad loves to look at fresh flowers.

There was one more thing I wanted to do.

"Does anyone know where the gift wrapping paper is?" I asked.

Mommy and Seth could not find it. So I made my own. I wanted to wrap up the videotape of my movie for Grandad before he came home.

I took plain white paper and decorated it with crowns, feathers, and balloons. (There were no balloons in my movie. But balloons on gift paper are very pretty.)

Finally everything was ready. We were

just in time, too. Granny was beeping the horn on the pickup truck outside.

"He is here! He is here!" I called.

We all rushed to the door at once.

"Welcome home, Grandad!" we said.

Grandad waved to us from the truck. He had a big smile on his face. But he hardly looked like my grandad. He looked smaller. And tired. I did not understand. I thought hospitals were supposed to make a person better.

Seth helped Grandad out of the truck and into a wheelchair.

I ran to Grandad and threw my arms around his neck. He felt awfully skinny.

"We are going to make you a big dinner tonight," I said. "If the hospital food was anything like the food on the airplane, you must be hungry!"

Grandad laughed. As soon as he did, he looked like Grandad again.

"It is so good to be home with my family," he said.

82

Seth wheeled Grandad into the house and helped him into bed.

"My goodness, this room is beautiful," said Grandad. "You all must have worked very hard. Thank you."

"Are you feeling tired?" asked Seth. "Would you like us to leave you alone so you can rest?"

"Leave me alone? No, sir. I want to visit with my grandchildren! I have missed them," said Grandad.

Andrew and I pulled two chairs next to Grandad's bed. We talked with Grandad. Then we played games. We even read him a story.

Grandad was finally home. Hooray!

The Gift

At five o'clock Tia arrived. We were having a welcome-home dinner party for Grandad, and Tia was invited.

Everything was ready. We were waiting for Grandad to wake up from his nap.

"Hello! Anybody home?" called Grandad from the den.

I ran in and gave Grandad a kiss. Then Seth helped Grandad out to the couch in the living room. We were going to have our party there because Grandad was too tired to sit up at the table for dinner.

All the food was spread out in the kitchen. There was roast chicken, corn on the cob, cooked zucchini with onions and snow peas, and a gigundoly beautiful salad. (Guess who made it.) We could put anything we wanted on our plates.

"If you do not like this food, we can call the hospital and see if they deliver," said Seth.

Grandad laughed. That is because he said the food at the hospital was terrible.

Clink, clink. Grandad tapped his spoon on his glass.

"I would like to say a few words," he said. "This is a very happy day for me. I am happy to come home to my wonderful family. I am happy our good friend, Tia, could be here with us. Karen and Andrew, thank you for flying all the way to Nebraska to see your old grandad. And thank you all for this beautiful homemade meal."

Our party was so much fun. We talked and laughed and ate and ate. Grandad had two helpings of my salad. I had two helpings of blueberry pie. (Tia and her mommy made it for us.)

After dinner, Grandad was feeling tired again so Seth helped him back to the den and into bed. The rest of us went along to keep him company.

"Excuse me," I said. "I will be right back."

I ran upstairs and got my gift. I brought it into the den and handed it to Grandad.

"This paper is so beautiful," said Grandad. "I wonder what is inside."

He carefully opened the package. Then he smiled.

"Grandad, this is my gift to you. I worked very hard on it and I hope you enjoy it," I said.

I popped my movie into the VCR and pressed the button marked "play." I saw myself on the screen. Then I heard myself speak.

" *Princess Gigglepuss* by Karen Brewer with a little help from her friends, Hannie and Nancy.' "

"I am in the movie, too," said Andrew.

"Quiet please," I said.

We watched the movie. At the end, everyone clapped. Grandad gave me a big hug.

"Thank you, Karen. I love my gift," he said.

"It was wonderful!" said Mommy.

"I wish I could have been in your movie," said Tia. "It must have been so much fun to make."

"Think of all the cooperation it must have taken," said Granny.

Cooperation? Hmm. I guess there had not been too much of that. I was glad Tia had not been in my movie. If she had been, she probably would not be talking to me anymore.

Nobody saw the extra parts that Bobby had filmed. They would have seen how bossy I was. They would have seen me talking like a big shot and not listening to anyone. I started to feel bad. My friends were all mad at me and I knew why. I had to do

something to make it up to them, and I knew just what.

Grandad was having a very good time at his welcome-home party. My friends like parties, too. I decided to give a party for them to thank them for being in my movie. I would give it as soon as I got home.

Making Plans

It was Sunday. It was time to say good-bye to Granny and Grandad. I hated to leave them.

"Call us when you get home," said Granny.

"If we do not answer right away, it is because we are busy watching our movie," said Grandad with a smile.

There were hugs all around. Then we went outside to meet Tia and her parents. They were going to drive us to the airport so Granny would not have to leave Grandad alone.

"I wish you did not have to leave so soon," said Tia.

"Me, too," I replied. "But I will be back. And I promise to write."

I felt sad about leaving Tia, but I was looking forward to getting home. I missed Hannie and Nancy. I wanted to give my party for them and for my little-house friends.

While we were on the plane, I asked Mommy and Seth if I could have the party. They said yes. They even said they would help if I wanted them to. Seth offered to make the snacks. Mommy said she would think of some games we could play.

As soon as we got home, I went to work making plans. First I wrote out a guest list. There were eight of us, counting me. Oh, yes. There was Midgie. She did not make it into the movie. But she had always showed up for rehearsals. That made nine. And Rocky would probably come whether

I invited him or not. So I put him on the list, too. Ten guests.

Next I thought about things we could do at the party. The most important thing was for everyone to see the movie. It would be just like opening night for famous movie stars. That was it! This was an Opening Night Party.

We would have snacks and play games. Then we would watch the movie. Maybe I would make a speech because I was the director. No. Maybe it would be better if I did not make a speech. I think my friends had heard enough speeches from me while we were making the movie.

I needed to think of one more thing. I wanted to find a special way to thank my friends. I sat in my room and wondered what that special thing should be. Hmm . . .

The Party

The party was on Wednesday night. Right after dinner the doorbell started ringing. My guests ran inside. They found the house decorated with streamers and balloons. Seth had made his excellent brownies. There was punch to drink, plus popcorn and plenty of snacks.

"Who wants to play Draw a Movie Star?" I asked.

This was one of the games Mommy had made up for the party. When she explained the rules, everyone wanted to play.

We divided up into two teams. I was on a team with Hannie, Nancy, and Andrew. On the other team were Bobby, Alicia, Kathryn, and Willie.

Mommy taped two big pieces of paper to the living room wall. She drew an oval on each one. The kids on each team lined up. When Mommy said, "Go!" we were supposed to take turns drawing a face and hair. The first team to finish drawing the movie star won the game.

"On your mark, get set, go!" said Mommy.

Hannie drew one eye. Nancy drew the other eye. Andrew drew a smiling mouth. When it was my turn, I drew hair. We kept going until we had drawn eyes, nose, mouth, and ears. Our movie star was very funny-looking. But we finished first and won the game.

After that we had a popcorn hunt and played musical chairs. Then I said, "It is showtime!"

I handed each of my friends a paper

bag filled with popcorn. When everyone had found a good seat in front of the TV, I popped the movie into the VCR and turned off the lights. We watched our movie and ate popcorn just like in a real movie theater. Everyone was very excited to see themselves on TV. We clapped at the end.

I wanted to show the movie again. But it was late and my friends were getting ready to leave. It was time for my surprise. I made a speech. But it was a teeny-tiny speech and I was not one bit bossy.

"Thank you for coming to my party," I said. "I know I could not have made this movie for my grandad without you. He really loved it. So now I would like to give each of you a thank-you present to take home."

My surprise was homemade movie posters. (I drew one poster and Mommy copied it for me at the post office.) I put the title at the top. Below the title was a picture of a giggling cat wearing a crown. I wrote the

names of the stars in alphabetical order. Then I wrote, "Filmed by Bobby Gianelli." At the very bottom of the page in the smallest letters it said, "Directed by Karen Brewer."

I went to bed that night feeling very happy. My friends liked their surprises and they were not mad at me anymore.

"That is the way it is with friends, Goosie," I said. "Sometimes you get mad at each other. But then you make up."

Before I fell asleep, I had a very good idea. Since this movie was such a big hit, maybe next summer we could make the sequel. I could see the poster now.

Princess Gigglepuss, Part Two—
Coming Soon to a Theater Near You!

PRINCESS GIGGLEPUSS

STARRING

KATHRYN BARNES * WILLIE BARNES *

ANDREW BREWER * NANCY DAWES *

ALICIA GIANELLI * HANNIE PAPADAKIS

FILMED BY BOBBY GIANELLI

DIRECTED BY KAREN BREWER

About the Author

ANN M. MARTIN lives in New York City and loves animals, especially cats. She has two cats of her own, Mouse and Rosie.

Other books by Ann M. Martin that you might enjoy are *Stage Fright*; *Me and Katie (the Pest)*; and the books in *The Baby-sitters Club* series.

Ann likes ice cream and *I Love Lucy*. And she has her own little sister, whose name is Jane.

Little Sister

Don't miss #64

KAREN'S LEMONADE STAND

Next I went upstairs and made a beautiful sign with great big letters in different colors. I drew a border of lemons all around. The sign said, *Karen's Lemonade, 10¢ a cup*.

There were only a few things left to do. I dragged a card table outside.

"Are you okay down there?" called Nannie.

(I had bumped into a few walls on the way out. I guess Nannie thought the house was falling down.)

"I am okay," I replied.

I carried out a chair. I brought out napkins and cups. I taped my beautiful sign to the table. Finally I carried out my ice cold pitcher of lemonade.

I sat down to wait for my first customer. This was my grand opening.

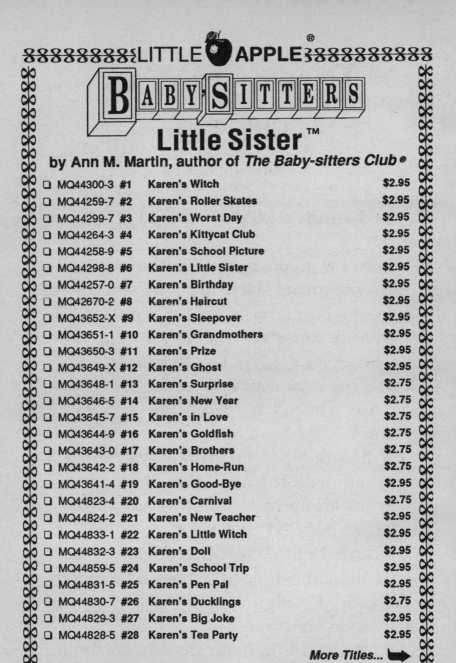

LITTLE ❦ APPLE

B·A·B·Y·S·I·T·T·E·R·S
Little Sister ™
by Ann M. Martin, author of *The Baby-sitters Club* ®

☐	MQ44300-3 #1	Karen's Witch	$2.95
☐	MQ44259-7 #2	Karen's Roller Skates	$2.95
☐	MQ44299-7 #3	Karen's Worst Day	$2.95
☐	MQ44264-3 #4	Karen's Kittycat Club	$2.95
☐	MQ44258-9 #5	Karen's School Picture	$2.95
☐	MQ44298-8 #6	Karen's Little Sister	$2.95
☐	MQ44257-0 #7	Karen's Birthday	$2.95
☐	MQ42670-2 #8	Karen's Haircut	$2.95
☐	MQ43652-X #9	Karen's Sleepover	$2.95
☐	MQ43651-1 #10	Karen's Grandmothers	$2.95
☐	MQ43650-3 #11	Karen's Prize	$2.95
☐	MQ43649-X #12	Karen's Ghost	$2.95
☐	MQ43648-1 #13	Karen's Surprise	$2.75
☐	MQ43646-5 #14	Karen's New Year	$2.75
☐	MQ43645-7 #15	Karen's in Love	$2.75
☐	MQ43644-9 #16	Karen's Goldfish	$2.75
☐	MQ43643-0 #17	Karen's Brothers	$2.75
☐	MQ43642-2 #18	Karen's Home-Run	$2.75
☐	MQ43641-4 #19	Karen's Good-Bye	$2.95
☐	MQ44823-4 #20	Karen's Carnival	$2.75
☐	MQ44824-2 #21	Karen's New Teacher	$2.95
☐	MQ44833-1 #22	Karen's Little Witch	$2.95
☐	MQ44832-3 #23	Karen's Doll	$2.95
☐	MQ44859-5 #24	Karen's School Trip	$2.95
☐	MQ44831-5 #25	Karen's Pen Pal	$2.95
☐	MQ44830-7 #26	Karen's Ducklings	$2.75
☐	MQ44829-3 #27	Karen's Big Joke	$2.95
☐	MQ44828-5 #28	Karen's Tea Party	$2.95

More Titles... ➡

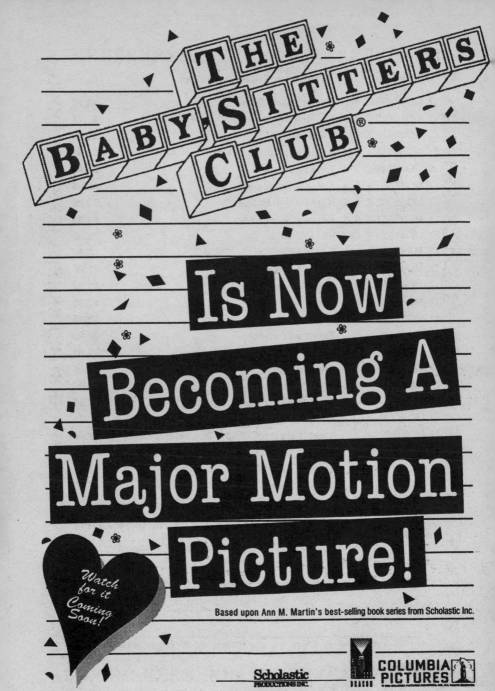

THE BABY-SITTERS CLUB®

Is Now Becoming A Major Motion Picture!

Watch for it Coming Soon!

Based upon Ann M. Martin's best-selling book series from Scholastic Inc.

Meet some new friends in a brand-new
series just right for <u>you</u>.
Starring **Baby-sitters Little Sister**
Karen Brewer...
and everyone else in the second grade.

Look for THE KIDS IN MS. COLMAN'S CLASS #1: TEACHERS PET.
Coming to your bookstore in September.

Now THE BABY-SITTERS CLUB.

★ is a Video Club too! ★